OLIVIA™
A Special Day with Dad

by Natalie Shaw
illustrated by Shane L. Johnson

Simon Spotlight
New York   London   Toronto   Sydney   New Delhi

Based on the TV series OLIVIA™ as seen on Nickelodeon™

SIMON SPOTLIGHT
An imprint of Simon & Schuster Children's Publishing Division
1230 Avenue of the Americas, New York, New York 10020
OLIVIA™ Ian Falconer Ink Unlimited, Inc. and © 2014 Ian Falconer and Classic Media, LLC
For information about special discounts for bulk purchases,
please contact Simon & Schuster Special Sales at 1-866-506-1949 or business@simonandschuster.com.
Manufactured in the United States of America 0314 LAK
First Edition 1 2 3 4 5 6 7 8 9 10
ISBN 978-1-4424-9751-1
ISBN 978-1-4424-9752-8 (eBook)

It was morning in Olivia's house, but something was different: It was quiet! When Olivia came downstairs for breakfast, she got a big surprise. . . .

Dad was the only one sitting at the breakfast table!

"Good morning, sweetie," he said, in between bites of cereal.

"Hi, Dad!" Olivia said, looking around for her mom and brothers. "Where is everyone?"

Dad explained that Mom, Ian, and Baby William went to run errands and go to Ian's soccer game. "So, today is a special day, just for you and me," Dad said. "What should we do?"

Olivia and Dad were full of ideas.
They could go to the amusement park.
They could go to the library.

They could go to the park.
But they couldn't decide what would be special enough for their very special day.

"I have an idea," said Dad. "I know you love seeing beautiful paintings as much I do. Let's go to the museum!"
Thinking of paintings gave Olivia another idea. "Let's make our *own* paintings!" Olivia said. "I have a new set of paints in my room."

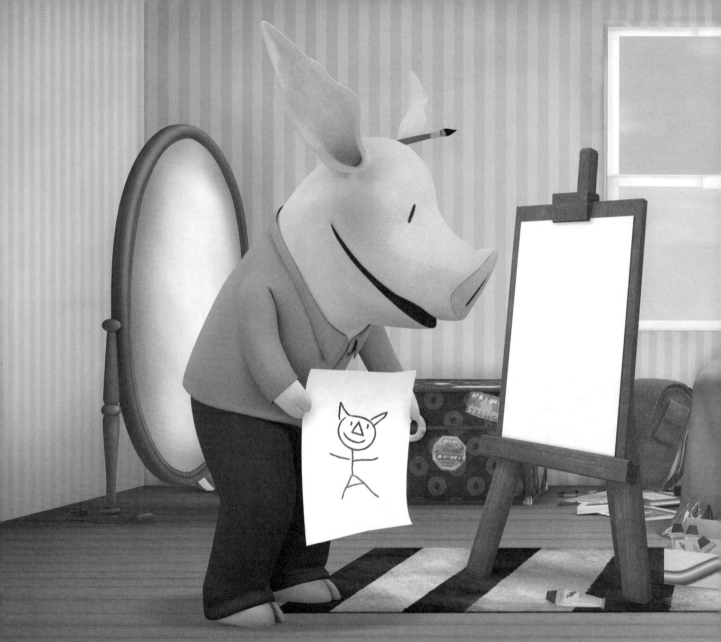

In Olivia's room, Olivia and Dad painted portraits of each other!

"It looks just like me," said Dad.

"It doesn't look just like me, exactly," Olivia said, "but I love it anyway."

They each signed their paintings and hung them up on Olivia's bedroom wall.
"What should we do next?" asked Dad.
"It's your turn to choose something, since I chose painting!" Olivia replied.

Dad decided that he would like to take Olivia to see the house he was building. "But before we go, I'd love for you to see the design for the house," Dad told Olivia, showing the plans to her. "The clients said they like gardening, but I don't think there is room for a garden."

Olivia and Dad looked at the blueprint together. "What if you added planters for flowers on the porch?" Olivia suggested. Dad thought it was a great idea! "Maybe I'll be an architect when I grow up, just like you!" Olivia told her dad.

Before long, it was time for lunch. Dad asked Olivia where she wanted
to go to eat.

"Where do you want to go?" Dad asked.

"Where do *you* want to go?" Olivia replied.

They both wanted to go somewhere that would be special for both of them!

"Okay," said Dad. "On the count of three, let's say what we want to eat.
One . . . two . . . three!"

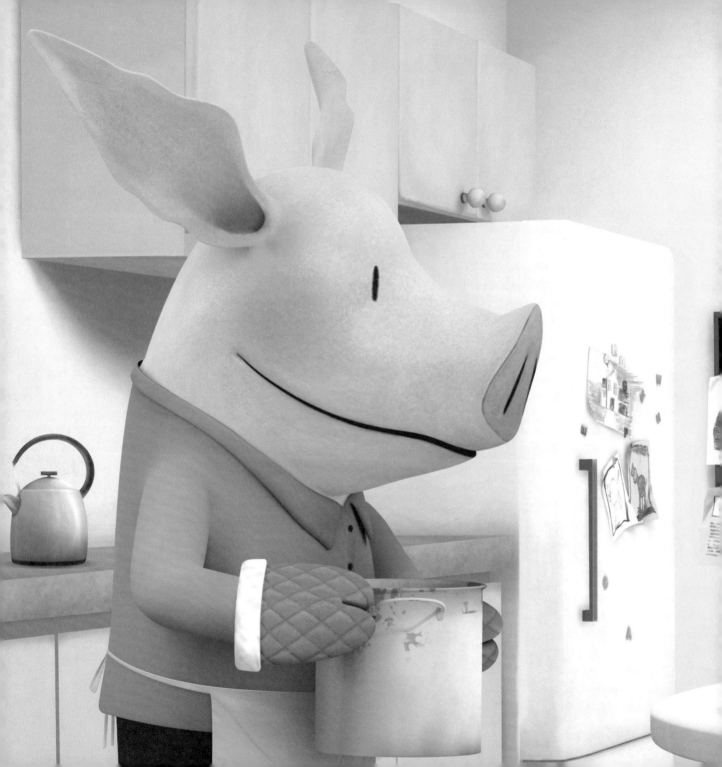

At the same time, Dad said, "Spaghetti," and Olivia said, "Pancakes." They didn't know of any restaurants that served both.

"Let's *make* lunch!" Olivia suggested. "That way it will be just what we want!"

Olivia helped Dad make the pancake batter and sauce. Then they sat down to their homemade daddy-daughter lunch. It was delicious!

When they were done eating, Dad told Olivia that the day was almost over and that they should go *somewhere*.

"We haven't left the house all day!" Dad said. "How about we go see that new movie about the dancers?"

"Wait! That reminds me," said Olivia. "I wanted to show you what I learned at ballet class this week!"
She put on her tutu and twirled and leaped all through the living room. Dad gave Olivia a standing ovation.

"Now it's your turn to dance!" Olivia told Dad.

"Well, I guess I do like dancing to oldies music," said Dad. So he put on one of his favorite songs and taught Olivia to do the Twist.

"I like this dance!" Olivia said, twisting to the music.

"So do I," said Dad, "but not as much as I like you!"

They were still dancing when Mom, Ian, and Baby William came home.

"Where did you go for your special day?" Mom asked.

"Nowhere!" Dad and Olivia said at the same time.

"And it was the best, most special day ever!" Olivia added.

Then Mom and Ian—and even Baby William—joined the dance party!

That night, at bedtime, Dad tucked Olivia in.

"Thanks for a special Daughter Day," Dad said.

"Thanks for a special Dad Day!" said Olivia.

Then they *both* fell asleep. It had been a very long, very fun, very special day!